THE PEANUT GARDEN

Created by Kenn Viselman

Written by Catherine Lyon and Scott Stabile

HarperEntertainment

An Imprint of HarperCollins*Publishers*

HarperCollins books are available at special quantity discounts for bulk purchases for sales promotions, premiums, or fund-raising. For information please write: Special Markets Department, HarperCollins Publishers Inc., 10 East 53rd Street, New York, NY 10022.

ISBN 0-06-054836-3

HarperCollins®, ®, and HarperEntertainment™ are trademarks of HarperCollins Publishers Inc.

First printing: May 2003

Visit HarperEntertainment on the World Wide Web at www.harpercollins.com

10 9 8 7 6 5 4 3 2 1

Dear Parents:

The most wonderful thing in children's lives is the love they receive from their families. Children derive tremendous pleasure from imitating their parents' care in pretend play and make-believe.

The Li'l Pets in Healy Fields are much like young children in their high spirits, rambunctiousness, and curiosity, as well as in their need to be loved and nurtured. They spend their days playing games, sharing stories, and exploring the world around them. When the adventures are just too much for the Li'l Pets to handle by themselves, the delightful Dr. Foxx is always there to fix their boo-boos and make them feel well and happy again. Then all they need is a li'l extra love from you.

Welcome to the loving and lovable world of the Li'l Pet Hospital!

With all good wishes,

Kenn Viselman

Stomp the Elephant sat quietly in the office at the Li'l Pet Hospital. His lower lip quivered as he tried hard not to cry. Dr. Foxx gently examined Stomp's trunk.

When he was finished, Dr. Foxx said,

"It's three large thorns that cause
*   the pain,*
But I will make you well again.
I'll take them out. It won't take long,
If you can just sit still; be strong."

Stomp took a deep breath. "Okay,
Dr. Foxx. Go ahead." Stomp closed
his eyes tight.

Dr. Foxx gave him a pat on the head
and went to his cupboard. He pulled
out a bottle of alcohol, some cotton
swabs, and a large pair of tweezers.

Dr. Foxx washed Stomp's sore trunk. Then he said,

"The painful part, I have no doubt,
Will be when these three thorns come out.
Think happy thoughts, relax, breathe deep.
Perhaps you'd even like to sleep."

Stomp squeezed his eyes shut even tighter. "Think happy thoughts, relax, breathe deep. Think happy thoughts, relax, breathe deep."

Soon Stomp began to daydream. He thought of his garden, the most beautiful place in Healy Fields. He remembered how it first began . . .

Stomp loved to eat peanuts. Often, when he munched on them, some would spill on the ground.

One morning Stomp noticed some strange plants growing in his yard. He decided to pull them up. He found lots of tiny peanuts clinging to the roots. Stomp got very excited.

He went to show his friend, Cutie Pie the Giraffe. "Look what's growing in my yard!" he said.

"Oh my!" she said. "You have a peanut garden! The perfect thing for an elephant!"

Stomp went back to his yard. There were *five* peanut plants. He decided to pull up all the weeds around them and to give the plants some water. Stomp began to work in his garden every day. Cutie Pie gave him a lovely straw hat so that he wouldn't get a sunburn.

Loveblossom the Pony and Splint
the Bunny found twigs and branches
and built a fence around the garden.
It even had a gate with a latch.

Limit the Puppy and Dropsie the Bear Cub loved to dig up the dirt and turn it over. Filo the Lion Cub made a big pitcher of lemonade for Stomp to drink when he got hot and thirsty.

Scuffs the Kitten came to watch. She often had her morning wash in the shade of a nearby tree.

One afternoon, Scuffs appeared carrying a large red flower in her mouth. "This beautiful flower will be good for the garden, too," she purred as she handed it to Stomp. "But be careful of the thorns. They're sharp."

Stomp was delighted! He carefully took the flower in his trunk and dug a small hole for it at the edge of his garden. It looked beautiful.

A few days later, the flower began to wilt. Stomp pulled up stray weeds around it. He watered it. Nothing worked. The flower's petals fell off one by one.

Stomp was very sad and missed the beautiful flower. He continued to take care of his peanut garden, but it wasn't the same.

In the fall, Stomp harvested his peanut crop.

Filo roasted the peanuts and made peanut butter. Then he made peanut butter cookies, peanut butter bread, peanut butter chili, and even peanut butter pizza. By the time winter came, none of the Li'l Pets wanted to see another peanut for a long, long time.

As the snow fell, Stomp remembered
the large red flower with the
beautiful scent.

Spring came, and one morning there was a knock at Stomp's door. Dropsie and Limit were standing outside, covered with dirt.

"Stomp," barked Limit excitedly. "We started digging and we found a new plant! Come on! Come look!" He barked and jumped around in circles.

"Let me get my hat," answered Stomp.

Dropsie and Limit dashed ahead of him. "Look! Look!" barked Limit. Stomp looked. There, where the red rose had been, was a small but sturdy plant.

24

On the branches were tiny buds and even
tinier thorns.

A few weeks later the buds on the small bush bloomed into beautiful red flowers. All spring and summer long the roses grew.

Late in the summer, the flowers all faded and fell. Stomp was sad to see them go, but now he knew that the roses would return every spring, just as his delicious peanuts did. The thought made him happy.

"Stomp, my very big brave friend,
The thorns are out; your pain should end.
Next time when you tend your rose,
Remember to protect your nose."

Stomp opened his eyes. There on his trunk was a large, snow white bandage. Dr. Foxx had removed the thorns and Stomp hadn't felt a thing!

And now all they need is

a li'l extra love from you!

Dr. Foxx says:

Gardening amid the flowers,

Makes us glad for many hours.

But be careful around roses.

Keep those thorns away from noses.

Now take your pet outside with you,

And let him smell a flower or two.